Saving Kate's Flowers

by Cindy Sommer

illustrated by Laurie Allen Klein

To Jordan,
Grow and bloom with reading and writing!
Cindy Sommer
2018

"Mom, why do flowers die in the winter?" asked Kate, tumbling in a leaf pile.

"It gets too cold for them outside," Mom said as she dragged a rake across the lawn.

"Can we bring them all inside?"

"That's a nice idea, honey. But we couldn't fit them all in our house." Kate's lower lip quivered. "We could save a couple."

Kate jumped up and down. "Thank you, thank you, thank you!"

Mom showed her how to use a shovel to scoop up a plant with its roots and put it in a pot. Kate helped pat down the dirt and give the plant water.

"Ooooh, can we save those?" she asked.

"Black-eyed susans come back next year," Mom said. "They're called perennials. Those over there are impatiens; they only bloom once. They're called annuals. We can save them."

They potted two impatiens.

"We'll take these seeds off the marigolds and dry them. Then we can plant them in the ground in the spring." Mom placed a few seeds into Kate's paw.

"I want those yellow ones too,"
Kate said, pointing to goldenrod.

They saved six more plants: two geraniums, three snapdragons and one goldenrod.

"Okay, that's enough," said Mom.

"Just a little more, please?" Kate asked.

The phone rang inside.

"I guess so. I've got to answer the phone."
Mom leaped into the house, carrying some
of the potted plants.

Kate grabbed more pots out of the shed. She dug, potted, patted, and watered until all the empty pots were full.

Mom still
talked on the
phone, hopping
back and forth in
front of the window.

Kate picked up an armful of flowerpots and carried them inside. She set a couple on the crowded windowsill and the rest on the kitchen table.

Mom whispered to her, "No more."

Kate held up two toes.

Mom nodded, and bounded into the living room.

Kate grabbed cups and bowls from the cabinets. She raced outside.

By the time Mom got off the phone, Kate had made several trips in and out of the house.

"How many more flowers did you save, honey?"

"A whole bunch."

"Really? Where are they?"

"I'll show you," said Kate.

"Oh my goodness!" Mom looked around Kate's room. Every dresser, shelf, and table was covered with flowers in bowls and cups.

"There's more in your room!" Kate hopped down the hall. "Doesn't it look pretty and smell like outside?" She sniffed.

"Yes, beautiful."

"Ah-choo!"

"That's Daddy!" Kate said,
rushing to the kitchen.

"What's going on here? Ah-choo!" said Dad.

"Hi, Dad," Kate giggled.

"Ah-choo! It smells like a garden." He hugged her.

"Wow! Where did all the plants come from? Ah-choo!"

"I'm saving all the flowers from dying," Kate said.

"That's very nice, honey. Ah-choo! But I'm allergic. Ah-choo!"

"Oh no. You'll have to sleep outside, Dad."

"I had a feeling this might happen, Kate," Mom said. "Dad has allergies. Come on, let's take these flowers outside."

"I'm sorry, Kate," Dad said. "All your hard work."

"Wait a minute . . . I don't want them to die!"

"Let's go outside and figure out what to do," Mom said.

Kate sat down on the front steps and sighed.

Mom gave her a hug. "What do you think we should do?"

Kate thought for a moment. "We could give one to Mrs. Chin next door." She jumped up. "And a bunch to the Hoppys, the Martin family, and Mrs. Pug."

"Great idea, Kate!" said Dad. "Ah-choo! I hope no one else is allergic."

"Mom, can I have some ribbon?"

Her mother hurried into the house and returned with red ribbon. Kate tied bows to each pot. They set them in a cardboard box on a wagon.

Kate and Mom delivered plants to their neighbors.

"Would you like to save a flower from the winter?
You would make it happy," she said to Mrs. Chin.

"Of course. Please give me two red geraniums."
Mrs. Chin smiled as Kate handed her the plants.

Mr. Hoppy chose two pink impatiens, and the Martins picked one begonia for each member of their family.

Mrs. Pug settled on three white New Guinea impatiens.

Kate and Mom gave away flowers to the rest of the neighborhood. Only the goldenrod remained.

"That can stay outside." Kate
looked up. "What about trees?"

"Don't even think about it," Mom said.

For Creative Minds

This section may be photocopied or printed from our website by the owner of this book for educational, non-commercial use. Cross-curricular teaching activities for use at home or in the classroom, interactive quizzes, and more are available online.

Visit www.ArbordalePublishing.com to explore additional resources.

Plant Parts

A

Like all living things, plants have different body parts that help them live, grow, and reproduce. Match the plant body part to its image. Answers are below.

B

Plants absorb water and nutrients through their **roots**. The roots are usually below the ground. They anchor the plant in place so it doesn't fall over or blow away. Some plants have very deep root systems. Other plants have shallow roots that branch out just under the surface.

The **stem** supports the weight of the plant. It holds the leaves and flowers off the ground. The stem connects the leaves and flowers with the roots.

C

Plants absorb sunlight through their **leaves**. They use the light's energy to make their own food. This process is called "photosynthesis." Leaves also have tiny holes that allow air to pass in and out of the plant.

Flowering plants need **flowers** in order to reproduce. Flowers make pollen. Wind, water, or animals (including insects) carry the pollen from one flower to another. When pollen from one flower lands on another of the same type of flower, that makes a seed.

D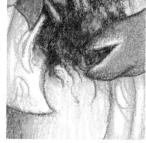

Plants have four basic needs:
- water
- air
- nutrients
- sunlight

What body part do plants use to take in water and nutrients from the soil?

Plants use their leaves to meet which two basic needs?

Which body part is used to create new plants (reproduce)?

Answers: A—flowers. B—leaves. C—stem. D—roots.

Life Cycle of Plants

Flowering plants have a life cycle, like all living things. Plants begin their lives as **seeds**. When the conditions are right to grow, a seed puts down roots to take in water and nutrients from the soil.

The **juvenile plant** has a shoot that starts to grow leaves. Plants need energy to grow. They get this energy from the sun, through their leaves.

As the plant grows, it becomes a **mature plant**. Like the juvenile plant, mature plants have roots, a stem, and leaves. They also grow flowers.

Flowers are how flowering plants reproduce. The flowers make seeds. When the conditions are right, the seed will put down roots and start to grow.

Some plants grow, produce flowers, and die all within one year. These plants are called **annuals**. Other plants may die in the cold months of winter, but regrow or return when conditions are right. These are **perennials**.

Which flowers in this story are annuals?
Which are perennials?

Potting Flowers

Do you want to save a flower from winter like Kate? It's easy. Just follow these steps:

1. Before it gets too cold, choose a small flowering plant to bring inside. Geraniums are a good choice. Even with the best care, some types of plants may not survive the whole winter. Make sure there are no bugs trying to hitch a ride with the plant. If there are bugs, a gentle squirt with a hose should take them off.

2. Take an empty pot that is made of plastic, rubber, or metal. Clay pots will dry out too fast. Be sure that the pot is a little larger than the plant. Make sure it has drainage holes. Place a saucer or a plate underneath the pot to catch the water.

3. Use a small shovel to dig in a circle around the plant, about 2 or 3 inches away from the stem. If you don't know how far that is, lay your hand flat on the ground against the stem, wrapping your thumb around it. The shovel should go along the outside of your hand, by your pinkie finger.

4. Scoop up the plant, making sure you leave dirt around the roots, and place it into the pot.

5. Add more dirt to the pot and pat it down to keep a snug fit around the plant.

6. Water your plant. Most flowers need to be watered a few times a week. A plant in a pot needs more water than one planted outside in the ground. But don't over-water it. If you poke your finger into the dirt, you can feel if it is wet or dry. Don't just feel the top; during winter the heat inside a building can dry the top of the dirt quickly. If half of your finger feels dry, you can water it. If it feels wet, check again in a day or two.

7. Place your plant by a window. Some plants need lots of direct sunlight, but others don't do well with too much light. Research your plant to find out its needs.

Follow these steps and your plant will be happy in its home for the winter. In the spring you can plant it back outside in the ground again.

Flower Identification

Can you identify the flowers in this book? Match the descriptions to the images of the flowers. Answers are below.

Marigolds have many layers of overlapping petals. The petals get smaller and closer together toward the center of the flower. They can be orange, yellow, maroon, red, or yellow-orange like the one shown here.

Impatiens have shiny, greasy leaves. The flowers are around 1 inch (2.5cm) long. There are many types of impatiens, like these pink ones.

Geraniums have large clusters of brightly colored flowers, each with five petals. The petals have veins running through them and can be white, pink, purple, blue, or red like the ones shown here.

Black-eyed susans have gold leaves around a brown cone. The flowers are about 4 inches (10cm) in diameter and the plants are 1-3 feet (30-100cm) tall.

Goldenrods can grow up to 3 feet (1 meter) tall. Small yellow flowers grow in thick clusters at the top of the stem. Goldenrod leaves are about 4 inches (10cm) long.

Snapdragons bloom on a central, vertical spike. They get their name from the flower shape that, when the sides are squeezed together, looks like a dragon's mouth. They come in many different colors, like these pink ones.

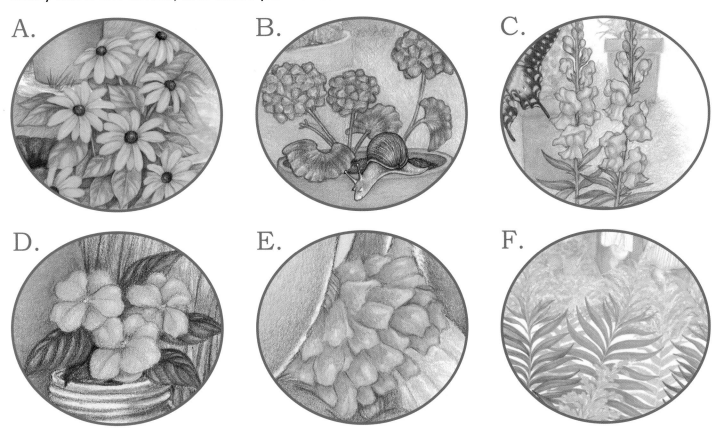

A.   B.   C.

D.   E.   F.

Answers: A-black-eyed susans, B-geraniums, C-snapdragon, D-impatiens, E-marigolds, F-goldenrod

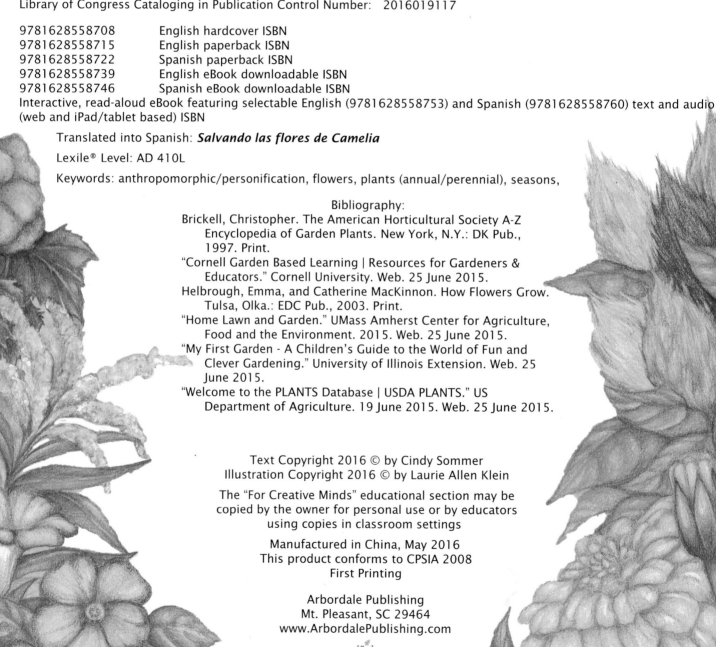

This debut book is dedicated with great joy to my husband, Robert, for supporting my writing all these years. Also to my two daughters, Samantha and Sabrina, who are my inspirations for many of my stories, including this one. I would like to thank my mother, Helga, for teaching me about flowers. Thank you to my father, Michael, for telling me to never give up, and to my friends and family for cheering me on. Thank you to my writer's group, the Long Island Children's Writers and Illustrators who patiently listened to my various stories and helped me to improve my writing skills. And the biggest thank you goes to you, the reader, who motivates me to write the best books possible.—CS

For Mom, and her extensive bunny collection, who introduced me to all the great rabbit stories. And for BK & JK, and all our friends and neighbors. I couldn't do it without you.—LAK

Thanks to Boxerwood Nature Center and Woodland Garden (Lexington, VA) for verifying the accuracy of the information in this book.

Library of Congress Cataloging in Publication Control Number: 2016019117

9781628558708   English hardcover ISBN
9781628558715   English paperback ISBN
9781628558722   Spanish paperback ISBN
9781628558739   English eBook downloadable ISBN
9781628558746   Spanish eBook downloadable ISBN
Interactive, read-aloud eBook featuring selectable English (9781628558753) and Spanish (9781628558760) text and audio (web and iPad/tablet based) ISBN

Translated into Spanish: *Salvando las flores de Camelia*

Lexile® Level: AD 410L

Keywords: anthropomorphic/personification, flowers, plants (annual/perennial), seasons,

Bibliography:
Brickell, Christopher. The American Horticultural Society A-Z Encyclopedia of Garden Plants. New York, N.Y.: DK Pub., 1997. Print.
"Cornell Garden Based Learning | Resources for Gardeners & Educators." Cornell University. Web. 25 June 2015.
Helbrough, Emma, and Catherine MacKinnon. How Flowers Grow. Tulsa, Olka.: EDC Pub., 2003. Print.
"Home Lawn and Garden." UMass Amherst Center for Agriculture, Food and the Environment. 2015. Web. 25 June 2015.
"My First Garden - A Children's Guide to the World of Fun and Clever Gardening." University of Illinois Extension. Web. 25 June 2015.
"Welcome to the PLANTS Database | USDA PLANTS." US Department of Agriculture. 19 June 2015. Web. 25 June 2015.

Text Copyright 2016 © by Cindy Sommer
Illustration Copyright 2016 © by Laurie Allen Klein

The "For Creative Minds" educational section may be copied by the owner for personal use or by educators using copies in classroom settings

Manufactured in China, May 2016
This product conforms to CPSIA 2008
First Printing

Arbordale Publishing
Mt. Pleasant, SC 29464
www.ArbordalePublishing.com